THE DREAMS
CAME TRUE

INTRODUCTION

As all have heard–"Every morning brings a new rise to a life."

Similarly, there was a girl named *Amelia*. She liked people who motivate the one who is getting demoralized. However, as she was from a lower class, all the people were disheartened. She did not like her society. As all the people of upper castes behaved them like they were the people from Earth. People demoralize the girls by saying them sentences like – Girls cannot study. Girls should be in kitchen, not in the fields.

However, Amelia was the girl who ignored these things and moved the steps of the world of equality and motivation.

In the beginning, she faced many problems but took them as a challenge. Further, you will see the challenges and tasks taken by Amelia. In addition, how she faced them. You will also see how the things changed and how it affected upper caste people and how she explored the world.

 At last, Amelia changed the life of her society. These all wee the dreams of Amelia to encourage the people of her society. Due to Amelia's efforts, she turned her dreams to truth.

CHAPTER-1

Amelia's mother, Luna wakes her and her brother up every morning at 5:30A.M. Luna asks her to draw water from the well and Mateo to study and then to work in the fields.

Sometimes, Amelia asks her mother, "Mom I want to study, may I." Nevertheless, always when she asks this question her father, Andrew stares Luna and she just answer, "Girls aren't made to study. Girls are made to do household work." Amelia always think that, why cannot a girl study? Why only a boy could study? Whenever she goes out of her home all the women starts staring at her. She felt very odd. Due to this, most of the times she enters her home back. However, sometimes she ignores and stays outside. She loved animals a lot and often plays with them. Nevertheless, on Sundays, she was not able to keep a step out of her home without her father's permission. If she gets out, her father scolded her very badly in the evening. So, she used to stay at home on Sundays.

As you know, she wanted to study. She watches her brother quietly and in this way, she was able to understand some of the words to read and write.

However, until now her parents were not aware about it. She was scared if her parents came to know about it.

Chapter-2

Amelia was also suffering with many problems in her society. It was noontime. Amelia was playing outside her home. Suddenly an irritating sound came, because of the sound all came out of their homes. All were worried, but Amelia was not because, in the morning when she went to draw water from the well, there was a large machine (J.C.B.) picking up the trees that were cut down by a man previous day. Nevertheless, there was no sound in the morning. Amelia asked Luna and went to see what is happening. When she came back and told that a rich man named Jack has come and is saying his companions for cutting down trees, as he wants to construct a huge building for his business. While she was saying, a woman interrupted in between and shouted loudly, "In the last society I had been living, the same thing happened and it took away all our homes. Therefore, my family had to leave it and settle here. I do not want to see the same as before." All were getting worried, but Amelia was giving them sympathy and saying, "Do not get worried, we should talk to them all will be fine." Nevertheless, no one heard her. When all were busy, she quietly went to Jack and asked her about all the doubts coming in the mind of her society.

After clearing all the doubts, she came back happily and announced, "We all are safe. The man told that we all are safe and there is no need to worry."

Chapter-3

As now, she wanted to explore the world and come out of stereotypes followed in her society. As you may have heard most of the people saying that, "If the cats cut the way and we move through something will go wrong." Amelia always think that why people believe in these stereotypes.

As she is a teenager should you that women have some natural processes within a month. During these days, she noticed that women are kept aside from everything. This is a natural process and it is not a women's fault.

She always wanted to find solution that why these things are done or we should not considered these types of stereotypes. This is why she wanted to explore the world. Amelia things that, "Instead of following the stereotypes people should give place and respect to them."

Now Amelia had decided that she would not follow these and she will make people believe that we should not follow these stereotypes her mother wanted to agree her but she do not have much confidence and positive attitude to come forward and speak. Therefore, she could not.

Chapter-4

Amelia was fed up of the thoughts of her society and their living style. Now she had decided that, after 5 days that is 2 January her 14th birthday, she would talk about it to her mother.

She decided to go away from her home and explore the world and its things new to her.

Two days were left for her birthday she was nervous and curious. She loves her family a lot and do not wanted to leave it. However, she also remembers all the problems and kept the stone on her heart. She remembered her dream to explore the world, to remove the thoughts of people believing on stereotypes, making a woman encourage and raising her society.

However, at the other side she was a child who has a melted heart. She was continuously thinking on it for 2 days. At a spot he also thought that, "why boys are given higher and more importance. Why the girls are demoralized?" 'It was enough', she thought.

Now it will be no more, this was the last she thought of her family. She decided that she will explore these things and she have to. We accept these as a challenge by nature to her.

Chapter-5

It was a morning with a new expectation and Sunshine. She woke up with a new expectation. She was waiting, since 5 days for this day.

Today her mother was happy, as it was her daughter's birthday.

However, Amelia was nervous about how she would speak, as her mother was so happy. She quietly went to her mother during noon. She said, "Mom I want a birthday present." Luna said, "What do you want my dear daughter?" Amelia said frightened of, "I...I...I... wanted... to... leave the home and explore the world."

Her mother remains quite with the great shock and did not say anything for a while. Luna eyes were filled with water and asked crying, "Why do you want this present, ask for anything else please."

Amelia said, "I wanted to do it before but, I also wanted to celebrate my birthday with you."

Luna could not say anything but after thinking about her daughter's dream. She cleans her tears, pretended to bold, and said strongly, "Yes, my dear daughter you may go. But how and when you will come back."

Amelia Boldly said, "I don't know when and how I will come. I just know what I can and I should do."

Amelia was nervous from inside but bold from outside. She hid all her tears inside her. Luna sadly packed the things in a blanket and said, "Promise me, you will do the things that you can do. You will not do anything in pressure."

She promised her mom and took her bag. She had just kept a step outside her home and a tear fell of her eyes.

She turned back, hugged her arms around the mother, kissed her, and ran away. When she ran away, her mother cried a lot...

When her father and brother came to know about it, they cried a lot and missed Amelia. Her mother said, "When she will come, she will come with change in the world."

Chapter-6

This was the first time Amelia went somewhere independently. She said to herself, "When I kept a step away from my home I realised as I was alone."

Nevertheless, when I reached out of my village, I found people helping the helpless people. Then I realised that I was not alone. Someone was with me for my help. I found that society talk only about selfish people not about selfless people. It was enough; I thought to be a selfless person not a selfish.

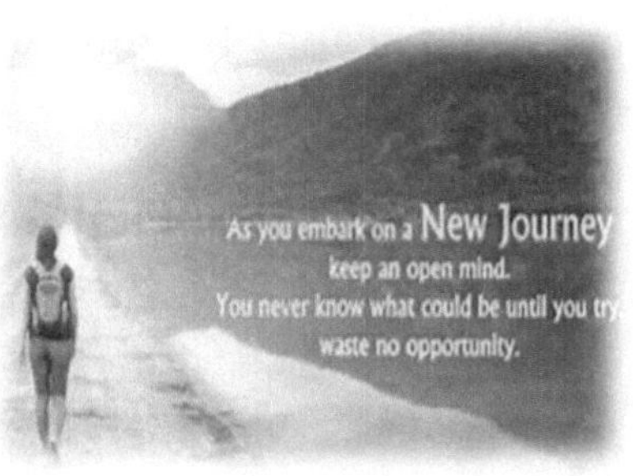

As Amelia walked through the way she realised that, the world is too large. It was her first day. She faced some problems, but solved those with others help. She was quite hungry, as she had eaten nothing after lunch. She saw in her bag that her mother had put some money. She counted those were 1500 rupees. She ate some food at a small cart of hawker. She loved that food but not more than her mother's hand made food.

This was the beginning of her journey.

Chapter-7

The life of Amelia was going on but her mind was still on her home. She thinks about her home when she faces problems. There were several problems; she solved them as a challenge. It was her second day; today she decided to find a home to live. She moved through to find a home for her or place where she could live. In the way, she met many fellows. In the beginning, she met an old man who was blind and walking with the help of a stick. In the front there was a car coming with high speed. A man came and saved the old man.

She also saw some selfish people but ignore them. As she walked through, she went to an old restaurant where no one lived. There was an old woman. When Amelia talked to her, she found that she was also from a nearby society. The old woman's name was Maria. She asked her that–"Hey my dear aunt, may I live here with you? However, I am sorry but I have nothing to give you accept my left over ₹1400. I wanted this money to buy things... but you may take it. May I please live here till I find a job and a new home?" Amelia said these words very politely. Aunt said, "Oh my dear princess, you may live here. I don't need anything from you."

Amelia was now happier than before, as she found a support with her to take her care.

Now she lived with her old aunt until she found a job, but other depends on her future. She founded easy because she accepted it as a challenge.

Chapter-8

Amelia was a smart girl. As she had learnt to read and write quietly from her brother, she got many advantages of it. She could read the signboards easily. In the beginning, she had faced problems in adjustment. She missed her family a lot.

Several thoughts came in her mind. She also thought that she should not leave her home. She also cried a

lot. See also ran a lot for the job, but no one gave her job after listening to her background. She joined her hands in front of everyone. No one allowed her. After much struggle, she opens the cart of handmade things that she had learnt from her mother. She took help of her old aunt.

In the beginning, she faced many problems in raising her business.

After 1 or 2 months, her business grew up a little. As her cart was rented and due to low business she could not fill it up. Their owners come to her every week.

After 2 months as much money she had she have to give it to the landowner, otherwise she could lose it. She faced many problems.

Chapter-9

Amelia's business was falling down. She got panic and confused. She did not know that what she should do. Her head was in a whirl. Amelia was thinking that she would die. One day in the morning when she was going with her cart, she saw some strange things. She saw that some people on the road were suffering from ailments due to lack of food. They were dying from hunger. She got inspired from them and took her business as challenge.

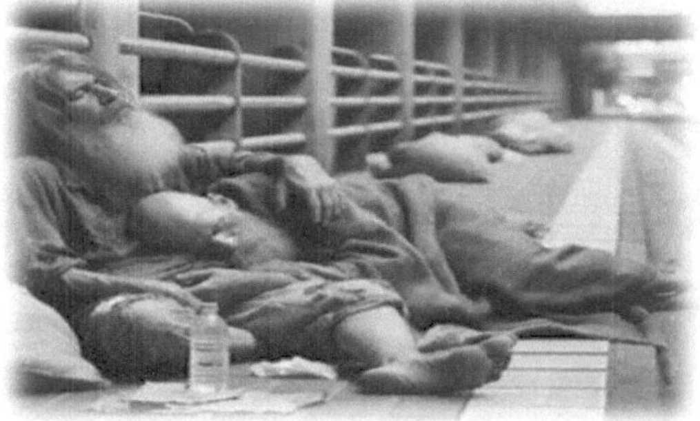

She put some efforts with her old aunt, Maria. This slowly reached to success and these efforts helped her in future.

This raised Amelia up and her income grew. Now she was able to be educated as her income grew up. After two months, there was Amelia's 15th birthday.

Chapter-10

Now Maria opens her cart and Amelia started to study in a government school. I love studying. She could catch easily that the teacher explains. However, children of her class dominate her and did not make her friend and treat so very strangely. She wanted to cry but does not. She accepted all the things. She just studies and go back home, do homework, and go for old aunt help and come back home with her aunt at 6:00 p.m... It also aunt to rest and cooks food. At 8:00 p.m., they eat food. Aunt sleeps before 9:30 and Amelia used to study until 1:00 a.m. to 2:00 a.m...

This routine showed effect in annual exams that were after 1 month. When the result was declared on the stage on 30 December, the first position and the school topper was Amelia with 99.8%... the second topper of was Roy with

94% in their class. He felt very jealous from Amelia and cried a lot.

Her aunt's eyes were filled with water of proudness. She had trophy and cash price of ₹15,000.

Interesting part was that Roy was of upper caste and his mind was thinking that his family member would not be happy with this...

Chapter-11

On 30 December, Amelia's whole day finished with result. Now on 30 December's night Amelia reminded  that her birthday is after two days that was 2 January. She went happily to Maria. She said, "Oh my dear aunt, it is my birthday after 3 days. I had promised my mother that I would be back on this birthday... Please let me go. If you do not feel bad, may I also take my... trophy with me that I received yesterday... If you could come... please come with me..." Maria did not want to leave Amelia but could not say no and said, "No Amelia I cannot come... you may go, your parents do not know me and will be waiting for you." Maria said these words to Amelia and turned around, and went to another room. Maria was carrying tears in her eyes. She cried a lot inside the blanket.

Amelia was happy because she thought that Maria was happy to see her happiness.

Another morning, Amelia got ready to leave for her home and aunt pretended to look happy and fed Amelia with her hands. While leaving, Maria gave her, her

Trophy and 15000 rupees she achieved, but Amelia just took trophy and 200 rupees for rent of travelling and trophy to show it to her parents. Now she was ready to leave. When she kept one-step outside her home, she turned in the same way just as she turned around to her mother one year before on her birthday.

She hugged Maria and started moving towards her home.

Chapter-12

Amelia was excited. As she caught the bus and reached, she saw many developments in the way. She was happy to see that. When she walked through and reached the gate of hers society she noticed some variations and saw that there are civilised people and there were *cemented* homes. When she went more inside the city, she could not find the any known person.

She asked a man, "Where are all the people who lived here and who are you?" He answered, "I am the owner of this city and all the people who lived here before are shifted 50kms from here before 9-10 months." Amelia was depressed and after hearing this, she was fainted. The man picked her up and took her to his home. She woke up at night and suddenly sat up as all of the man's family members were around her. She said with urge, "Who are you all", "Where are my parents?"

The man's wife asked her politely, "What is your parent's name and what is you doing here?" Amelia told all the things happened since last year.

Man's wife said, "May, we leave you there?"

Amelia said with hope, "Really, will you leave me?"

Man said, "Yes of course."

Amelia slept that night there and next morning they went to leave her in their own car.

Chapter-13

The distance was 50km. There were chances to reach their in approx. 1:30 hours... Amelia was excited but at the other side, her mother was alone at home and was crying. She was missing the last year when Amelia was with her and they were living happily. After one and a half hour, they reached Amelia's home. As Amelia stepped out of the car, her mother saw her and was confused to see Amelia. The man and his wife also came out of the car. Amelia's eyes filled with water and she ran towards her mother. Her mother also ran

towards her and they hugged tightly. They both cried a lot. The man and his wife were happy to see them together. They took them inside their home and Luna asked them to stay with them. The man told all the things happened. Luna said, "Oh Amelia, how much you have changed. Your behaviour, your  way of talking, your style of doing work and perfection in each work..."

The wife said, "Ok Amelia, now you seemed to be happier. Shall we leave now?"

"No, why would you leave? Stay here with us." Amelia said.

The man said, "Yes sure, but next time. I have a small son. He might be waiting for us."

"Yes, you may go. Time is passing and you might get late. I again thank you to leave my daughter here." Luna said.

They went back. Amelia and Luna talked the whole day and Amelia showed all the prizes achieved by her in her school. She also told about the cash prize she got, how she found her home, how kind people are there in the world just like Maria aunt.

When Andrew and Mateo came, they were surprised to see Amelia after one year. Luna told her husband about the man and his wife who left Amelia in their car.

Chapter-14

It was a new sunshine with a great joy. It was Amelia's fifteenth birthday. She was full of excitement and happiness. All her family members missed her a very happy birthday.

Her mother now had learnt to make cake. She made a cake with fruits decorated on it. Andrew bought a small

gift for her, due to which Amelia got happier than before. In the evening whole family celebrated her birthday.

Andrew had brought a mobile phone from one of his friend to work. Amelia wanted to call Maria. She asked her father, "Father, may you give me this phone. I wanted to call Maria."

Andrew allowed her to call. She opened her diary in which she had contact numbers of Maria and some of the neighbours. She firstly dialled to Maria, 4-5 times but no one picked the call. She got worried and different thoughts came in her mind. She then dialled the phone to her neighbour, Eliza. She picked up the phone and without saying hello Amelia said, "Eliza di, where is aunt please check he." She said with a strange behaviour. "Yes sure, wait for a minute. Let me go." Amelia was tensed and when she heard Eliza's strange voice, she got confused and said, "Hello...Hello...Hello" but no response came and Eliza's phone fell down and

the call got disconnected.

Amelia was unable to think and was tensed and confused. She gave back phone to Andrew in a hurry.

She wanted to go back next day. She was having a high temperature that night. Next morning, when she woke up her parents asked, "What had happened to you?"

Chapter-15

Amelia answered, 'I wanted to go back. Yesterday aunt did not pick up the call."

Andrew said, "Yes sure, we will go back soon. This time we will also go along with you and meet her."

After two days, on 5 January, Amelia and her family started to move towards the city in a car on rent. They reached the city at 6:30 P.M. Amelia now guides her father to reach their destination. Upon Their arrival, they found the house unlocked... No sound was coming from inside.

Amelia slowly opened the door. She and her family went inside. Amelia shouted with the mystery, "Aunty, aunty where are you?" No response came. She was about to cry, but controlled. She went to her neighbour Eliza... She asked, "Di please tell me, where is aunt." Amelia said in a cried voice.

Eliza replied in a dumb voice, "She, she... is no more Amelia. She passed a day before you called due to heart attack..."

Amelia was shocked, went back crying to her mother, and told her that Eliza told to her.

They all cried a lot...

Chapter-16

Amelia was so sad after the expiry of Maria. Now her family started to live in the city only with Amelia. In addition, her family supported her a lot. Her father had found a job in which he earns ₹15000 per week. The cart used by Amelia and Maria was now kept at their home. Her brother was now studying at a good school.

After a few years after passing her 12th class, she joined a university and coaching classes.

Amelia wanted to crack neet exam, as she wanted to be a doctor. However, it needed a lot of preparation. In 2017, she gave her first attempt but could not clear but her family held her and supported her. Her brother had cracked the exam of SSC.

In 2019, one year before the spread of Covid-19. She had prepared a lot for it. It was too tough to express her views. She was also too nervous. She gave exam with as much confidence as much she could. She was of 28 years. She also thought that if she could not clear this time she would not try again. Her father had also said that her age is now going on. Now, she had to marry also.

It was 11 August 2019; you went to the centre to give exam. After 3 or 4 months, a strange call came to her.

She picked up the call and answered, "Yes, myself Amelia."

A computer voice came, "Congratulations you have cracked your NEET exam 2019."Moreover, the phone disconnected.

She was confused, went to her parents, and told this. All were proud of her and giving her many blessings.

After that in December, there was an interview for her job. She has worn sari and answered all the answers correct with full confidence.

On 2 January, she came to know that she had cleared. It was her best birthday present.

Now, she was a well-known doctor of PGI... She had tied a knot with an IAS officer and was joyfully raising two children. Her mother, father and brother were also living happily. Her brother was also married and was having a son.